RICKY KENNISON

AuthorHouse™
1663 Liberty Drive
Bloomington, IN 47403
www.authorhouse.com
Phone: 1 (800) 839-8640

Published by AuthorHouse 08/22/2016

ISBN: 978-1-5246-2594-8 (sc)
ISBN: 978-1-5246-2593-1 (e)

Library of Congress Control Number: 2016913800

Print information available on the last page.

This book is printed on acid-free paper.

authorHOUSE®

LILLEY
The Pizza Mouse

It was Wednesday evening December 24 and tucked away in a hole in the woods was Mr. and Mrs. Mouse. Mrs. Mouse was in the family way and she was eating on a root of Lily flower coming thru the ceiling. The hole in the ground was nice and warm and Mr. Mouse had helped bring some dried leaves in their home for a comfy bed.

Lilley was born the next morning on Thursday Christmas Day. She was a cute little mouse. Lilley's eyes were not open yet and she didn't have any hair. A little time passes and Lilley's eyes open and she became a soft furry little mouse. Lilley had a dark spot on the tip of her left ear. Lilley didn't have any sisters or brothers.

A few weeks pass and Lilley grows bigger. She spends all day playing games with her mother and father. As spring starts to come Lilley goes outside of her home in the ground to look at her surroundings. To Lilley's surprise she finds she lives in a wonderful place in the woods. Oh, how happy is she! What a joy for her to have the wonderful woods to play!

Lilley is full of happiness as she explores her woods. In the woods she finds leaves, twigs, trees, and plants. There's rocks to clime and clumps of dirt also. She has such a good time playing at her warm home in the woods.

Soon Lilley grows bigger and starts to find interesting things to eat: roots, bugs and maybe some flowers if they plume soon. She could try them if they plume. A mouse can eat flowers can't she? I mean if she wants.

Lilley's dark spot on the tip of her left ear gets bigger and bigger covering one half of her ear on the tip. Lilley sees herself in the water puddles and she thinks her dark spot on her ear is so beautiful. What a special mouse she must be!

Lilley keeps growing and getting bigger! Lilley goes further and further into her woods playing and having fun. One day she was playing in the woods and she hears loud noises. She goes to investigate the loud noises. Lilley finds a clearing in the woods with loud machines going back and forth. The machines were traveling back and forth on looked to her like a bed of rocks. She didn't know the machines were cars. She just knew they made lots of noise. Zoom goes the cars back and forth, what a lot of noise. Lilley didn't like the noise. The noise was too loud for her tiny ears. Even to loud for the ear with a dark spot. She didn't like this noise at all.

Lilley goes back home and tells her mother and father about the loud noises. Lilley says to her mom, "there is something in the woods that makes loud noises and zooms back and forth really fast." Her parents warn Lilley to stay away from the place that makes the loud noises. Sometimes when a mouse goes there they are never seen again. Lilley says. "yes mother I won't go there."

A few days passes and Lilley keeps going back to the place where the loud noises and the machines go by. Lilley can't resist. She goes out into the new place, and soon she is on the other side of the road and is afraid. Lilley keeps going and she finds lot of people and buildings. A party maybe Lilley thinks.

Lilley keeps going and all of a sudden she smells this wonderful smell. She follows her nose and the smell keeps getting stronger and stronger. It's a wonderful smell Lilley thinks. Finally, Lilley finds a building where people are busy going in and out. If Lilley could read the sign on this building would read Pizza. Yes, Lilley smells pizza from a Pizza Restaurant. Better yet Lilley smells pizza cheese.

PIZZA
CHEESE

Lilley sneaks in the Pizza Restaurant door as someone goes out. What a wonderful place, Lilley thinks to herself. Lilley decides to look around this new place. Lilley looks over every corner and what does she find? Boxes of pizza cheese. Lilley finds a small piece of pizza cheese on the floor and she carefully tastes it. It tastes good. Pizza cheese taste really good. So she starts eating pizza cheese and she forgets about going home to mom and dad. Lilley thinks to herself, "what a wonderful life! I can stay here and eat pizza cheese forever."

Soon someone comes in and sees Lilley. They take a broom and try to sweep Lilley away but Lilley runs and hides. Lilley thinks, "she must be careful eating pizza cheese or she might be seen and swept away by the boom."

PIZZA
PIZZA
PIZZA
PIZZA
PIZZA
PIZZA
PIZZA
PIZZA

While Lilley hinds from the broom she hears lots of voices talking. And, one voice says, "I'm the exterminator and my name is Ms. Cacher. I'm hear to spray for bugs and catch the mice." Lilley thinks, "what's an exterminator - another person with a broom?" It was a woman's voice and a woman exterminator to spray for bugs and catch mice. Lilley thinks, "she must not let Ms. Cacher see her or she will be swept away by the exterminator."

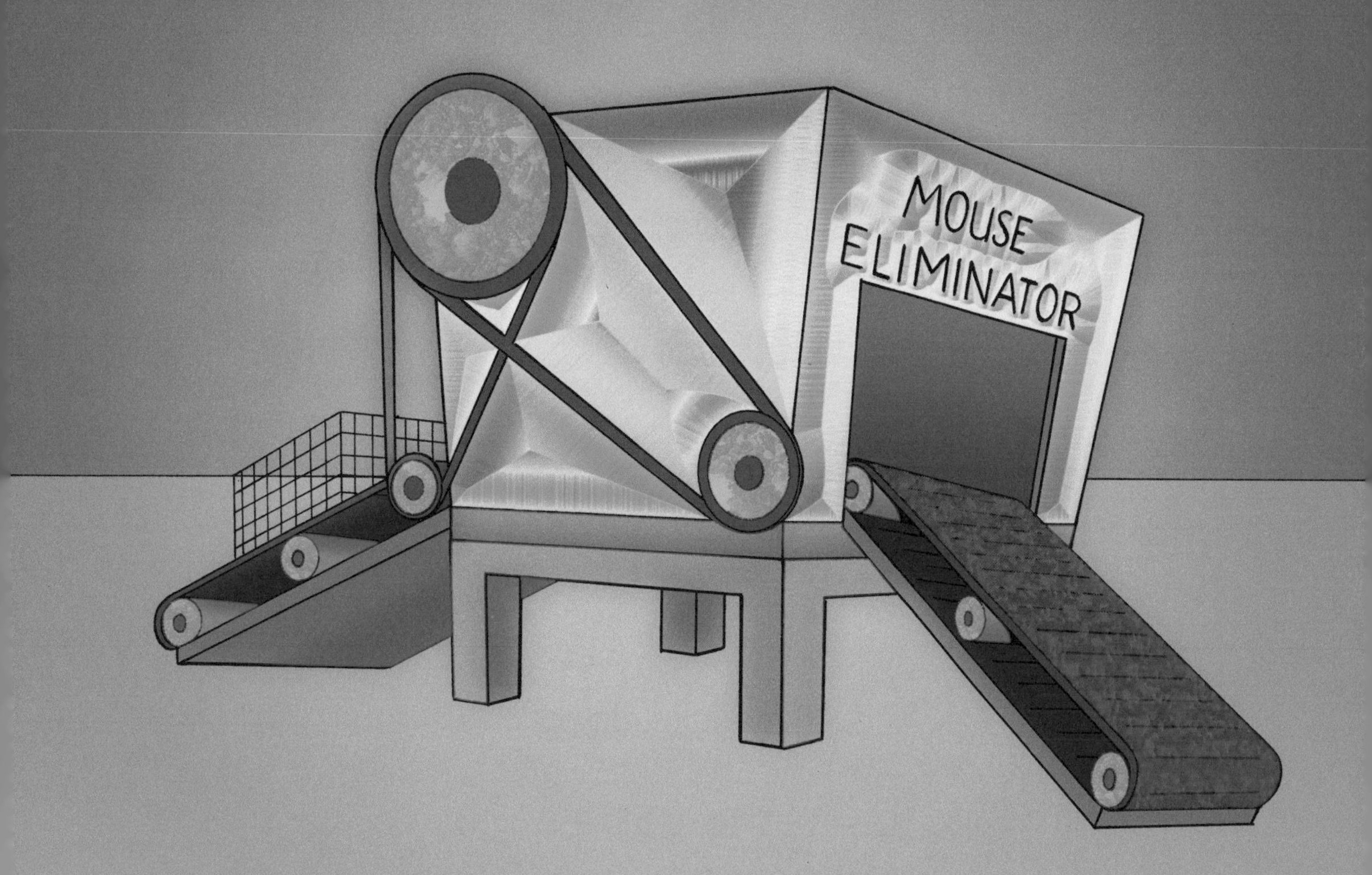
MOUSE
ELIMINATOR

Ms. Cacher tells the pizza restaurant owner, Mr. Tony Mazzorilli, about catching mice. Ms. Cacher says her company has a new machine - a mouse eliminator. She catches the mouse puts the mouse in a small cage. She sets the mouse and cage on the conveyor belt, that goes inside the Mouse Eliminator. When the cage comes out of the machine on the conveyor belt, there's no more mouse just an empty cage! The best mouse eliminator yet! "It works great, "says Ms. Cacher. "It eliminates the mouse!" Mr. Mazzorilli the pizza restaurant owner says, "great idea Ms. Cacher wish I had thought of it!"

Lilley hears all this conversation between Ms. Cacher and Tony, and she doesn't like it! Lilley tries to hide good from Ms. Cacher, and the broom too. Lilley went into hiding and only came out in the dark of the night. Lilley was so hungry from hiding all day waiting for night. She had to eat the pizza cheese. She couldn't help herself. Lilley thought the pizza cheese smelled and tastes so good. She ate a lot of it. She couldn't help herself.

MINATOR

One night when Lilly came out to eat the pizza cheese it was so dark everywhere except for one small light way down the hallway. Lilley could hardly see. Lilley carefully looked around and seen nobody. It was safe she thought. She came out to eat the pizza cheese except the pizza cheese was put away somewhere. Lilley couldn't find anything to eat. Lilley looked and looked. Finally, she smells pizza cheese, but it didn't look safe. It was just a small piece. It smells so good and Lilley was hungry. Lilley went closer. It seemed safe. Lilley stepped inside a little door. She could see the pizza cheese and it smelled good! Lilley went close to the pizza cheese carefully. Slam! Lilley heard a loud noise. Lilley looked behind her and the little door was shut. She was trapped! Lilley ran around in circles trying to get out, but she couldn't. Ms. Cacher had caught her in a cage! The lights came on and Ms. Cacher came to the cage and said, "I caught the mouse that was eating the pizza cheese. I'll take the cage and mouse to the Mouse Eliminator."

Lilley begged Ms. Cacher, "please don't put me in the Mouse Eliminator. Please don't do it! Please don't do it!" "I was so hungry and the pizza cheese was so good," Lilley says to Ms. Cacher. Lilley says to Ms. Cacher, "if you let me go I wouldn't eat anymore pizza cheese."

Ms. Cacher picks up the cage with Lilley inside and says, "I'll think about it tonight." Ms Cacher turns the lights back off and takes the cage with Lilley inside outside in the night air. Ms. Cacher puts the cage and Lilley inside the back of a truck, and shuts the top of the truck door. Lilley was so scared and it was so dark in the back of the truck. Lilley keeps saying, "let me go and I won't eat the pizza cheese anymore!"

It was Saturday night and what a Saturday night to remember, Lilley thought. The truck starts moving. What a bumpy ride it was, and dark in the back of the truck. The truck roared into the night. It was a long bumpy ride then the truck just stopped. It was all quiet and Lilley could her Ms. Cacher shut the truck door with a bang. Lilley was stopped. The truck was stopped. All was quiet again. Lilley was tired from the long ride in the back of the truck. She laid down and went to sleep.

Lilley woke in the morning when the truck door made a noisy. Ms. Cacher was back at the truck. Suddenly Lilley saw day light. Ms. Cacher had opened the door to the back of the truck while Lilley was still in the cage. It was Sunday morning (Easter Sunday). The air was cool but not cold. Ms. Cacher grabbed Lilly's cage and took it out of the truck with Lilley still inside. Ms. Cacher said to Lilley, "Now maybe you won't eat pizza cheese anymore." Ms. Cacher started waking carrying Lilley in the cage. She walked along a path next to the woods. Lilley was back in the country side again. She knew what the woods were like. Lilley used to live in the woods with her mom and dad in a hole in the ground. Ms. Cacher kept walking in the woods for a long time. Then, Ms. Cacher stopped and put the cage down on the ground. Ms. Cacher tells Lilley, "today is Easter Sunday so I am letting you go. Please don't come and eat the pizza cheese again!"

Lilley tells Ms. Cacher, "Thank You! Thank You! I wouldn't never go back and eat the pizza cheese again. Ms. Cacher opens the cage and Lilley goes out back into the woods. Soon Lilley recognizes she is back in the woods where she came from. The same woods. Lilley gets her directions. And, she finds the trail back to the hole in the ground where she lived with her Mother and Father. Lilley's Mother and Father greet her. "Lilley where have you been," say Lilley's Mother? Lilley answers, "it's a long story. I'm just glad to be back home again!" Lilley stays with her Mother and Father in the hole in the ground happily ever after.

"The road maybe filled with twists and turns but you can always go back home," Lilley thinks to herself!

The END.

Printed in the United States
by Baker & Taylor Publisher Services